The Strongest Mum

Nicola Kent

MACMILLAN CHILDREN'S BOOKS

For Martha and Harry, my super-strong,
treasure-spotting helpers.

With special thanks to Pam and Martin.

First published 2018 by Macmillan Children's Books
an imprint of Pan Macmillan
20 New Wharf Road, London N1 9RR
Associated companies throughout the world
www.panmacmillan.com

ISBN 978-1-5098-5231-4 (HB)
ISBN 978-1-5098-5232-1 (PB)

Text and illustrations copyright © Nicola Kent 2018

The right of Nicola Kent to be identified as the author and illustrator of this work
has been asserted by them in accordance with the Copyright, Designs and Patents Act 1988.

1 3 5 7 9 8 6 4 2

A CIP catalogue record for this book
is available from the British Library.

Printed in China

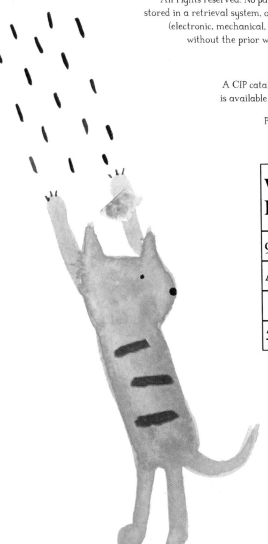

My mum is the strongest mum in the world.

WAHAY!

She's always been good at carrying things.
Which is great because I've always
been good at finding things!

Mum, can you carry this?

Can you carry this?

Can you carry these?

Come on.
Pop them in my bag.

There's always room for my treasures in Mum's bag.

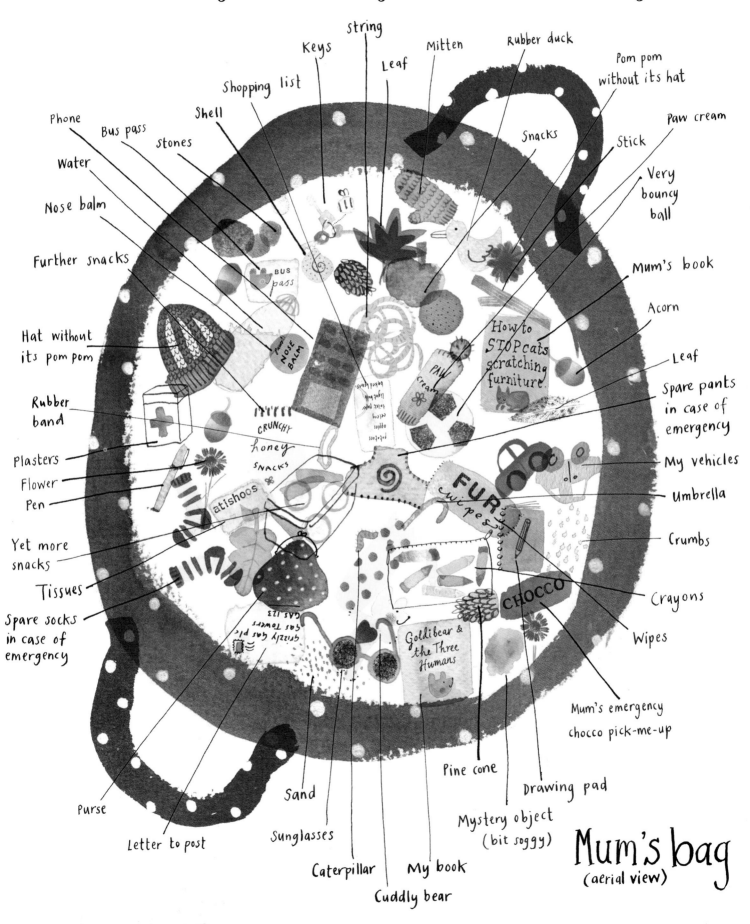

Mum's bag
(aerial view)

Mum got good at carrying
bigger and bigger things.

It wasn't that I didn't like my
bike. I just got tired sometimes.

REALLY tired.

My mum never got tired.

Mum was great at helping her friends, too.

Can you carry this?

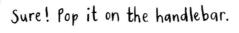

Sure! Pop it on the handlebar.

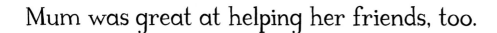

She carried Zebra's shopping,

Lion's laundry,

and Elephant's carpet.

Soon EVERYONE knew I had the strongest mum in the world.

Can you carry these?

Can you carry these?

Can you carry this?

She carried the lot. She even carried . . .

... Flamingo's piano!

Recipes

stories

yoga

Thanks!

KNEADS BREAD

WOW.

Mum probably had
enough to carry.

But it's not often you
find treasure THIS good.

Mum! Mum!
It's a triple header!

It was just one thing too many. My mum began to teeter and totter and wibble and wobble, until . . .

Are you ok?

My mum wasn't feeling very strong any more.

Don't worry Mum,
they're only things.

Mum's friends rushed to lend a hand.

Lion phoned a friend
who could fix pianos,

and Zebra
mended the bike.

Flamingo made a lovely soup
with all the broken veg,

while Elephant tidied up.

And I picked up the
treasure for Mum.

Everyone agreed she
deserved a good rest . . .

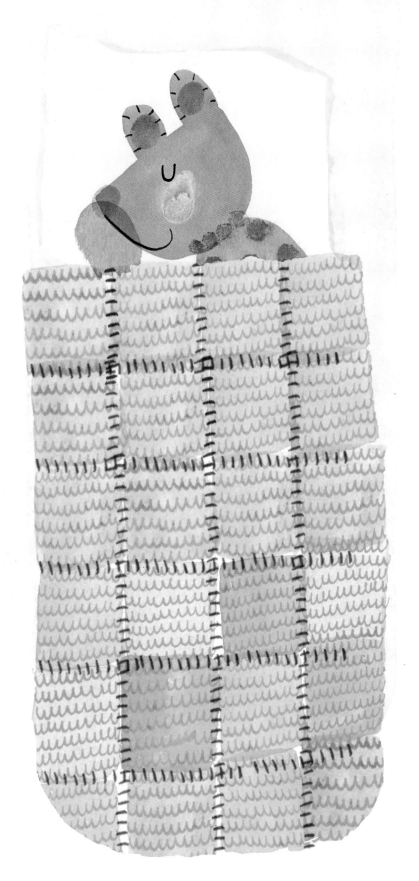

. . . and a bit more help.

How to
STOP cats
scratching
furniture.

It wasn't long before Mum
began to feel right as rain . . .

. . . and ready to get
going again.

Honey
BUBBLES

Tra la la

Quack quack

Glosso
Luxury
shampoo
for
shiny
ears

Purse, check.
Phone, check.
Keys, check.
RIGHT!

But first I wanted to give her some treasure of her own.

This is beautiful!

I made it just for you!

WAHAY!

My mum is the strongest mum in the world . . .

. . . and I'm getting super-strong too.

LEPHANT'S CARPETS

THE
FLICKS

Let's carry this
together.